Au

For Gavin—J. S.
For Dr. J. S. G. Simmons—R. A.

First published in the United States in 2002 by Chronicle Books LLC.

Text © 2001 by James Sage.
Illustrations © 2001 by Russell Ayto.
Originally published in Great Britain in 2001 by HarperCollins *Publishers* Ltd.

North American text design by Kristen M. Nobles.
Typeset in Farao and Greymantle.
The illustrations in this book were rendered in watercolor and ink.
Manufactured in China.

Library of Congress Cataloging-in-Publication Data
Sage, James.
[Fat cat.]
Farmer Smart's fat cat / by James Sage ;
illustrated by Russell Ayto.
p. cm.
Originally published: Fat cat. Great Britain : HarperCollins, c2001.
Summary: Farmer Boast, Farmer Bluster, and Farmer Smart fight over who has the best cornfield, until one
of them finds a way to win the competition.
ISBN 0-8118-3502-2
[1. Competition (Psychology)--Fiction. 2. Corn—Fiction. 3.
Cats—Fiction.]   I. Ayto, Russell, ill. II. Title.
PZ7.S1304 Far 2002
[E]--dc21
2001004061

Distributed in Canada by Raincoast Books
9050 Shaughnessy Street, Vancouver, British Columbia V6P 6E5

10 9 8 7 6 5 4 3 2 1

Chronicle Books LLC
85 Second Street, San Francisco, California 94105

www.chroniclekids.com

Farmer Smart's Fat Cat

By James Sage

Illustrated by Russell Ayto

chronicle books · san francisco

Farmer Boast lived next door to Farmer Bluster ...

who lived next door to Farmer Smart ...
and each thought his cornfield was the best.

"No doubt about it!" claimed Farmer Boast.
"My cornfield is the best!"

"It isn't!" argued Farmer Bluster. "My cornfield is
much better than yours."

Now, Farmer Smart knew that his cornfield was better than both of his neighbors', but he was much too modest to say so.

One day, much to the dismay of all three farmers, they discovered that mice had been eating the young corn.

To teach those mice a lesson they would never forget, Farmer Boast and Farmer Bluster each set out to build the perfect mousetrap.

They hammered and twisted and pushed and pounded away all day and most of the night and part of the next day, too.

"Those mice will soon learn who's boss around here!" bragged Farmer Boast.

"With my invention they don't stand a chance!" gloated Farmer Bluster.

And when they had finished, they just couldn't help sneaking over to inspect the other's mousetrap.

 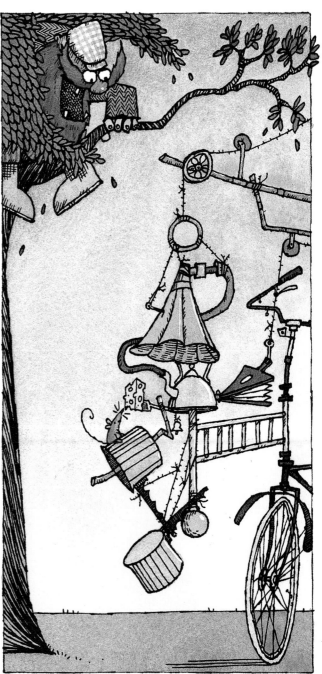

"What a piece of junk!" smirked Farmer Boast.
"He hasn't a clue!" snickered Farmer Bluster.

But there was one teensy-weensy problem that neither had considered. It seemed the mice weren't interested in either mousetrap.

Hurrah!

Check it out!

Let the good times roll!

They had better things to think about.

While the mice stuffed themselves, the cornfield of Farmer Smart remained strangely untouched.

Which is what they did.

And it wasn't long before they discovered the real reason behind Farmer Smart's amazing success at keeping the mice away.

Farmer Boast looked at Farmer Bluster, and Farmer Bluster looked at Farmer Boast, and they decided there and then to steal Farmer Smart's highly efficient mouse catcher.

So that our fields are mouseless, too!

They left no stone unturned, but Fat Cat was nowhere to be seen.

"Guess there's no way out of this one," muttered Farmer Boast.

"You can say that again!" sighed Farmer Bluster.

"Now, now, my friends, there's no need to feel so glum," said Farmer Smart. "I think what you may be looking for is over there, resting in the hay. Only she's not quite so fat anymore."

And sure enough, there was Fat Cat, much slimmer and very, very pleased with herself. KITTENS!" exclaimed Farmer Boast. A WHOLE LITTER!" gasped Farmer Bluster.

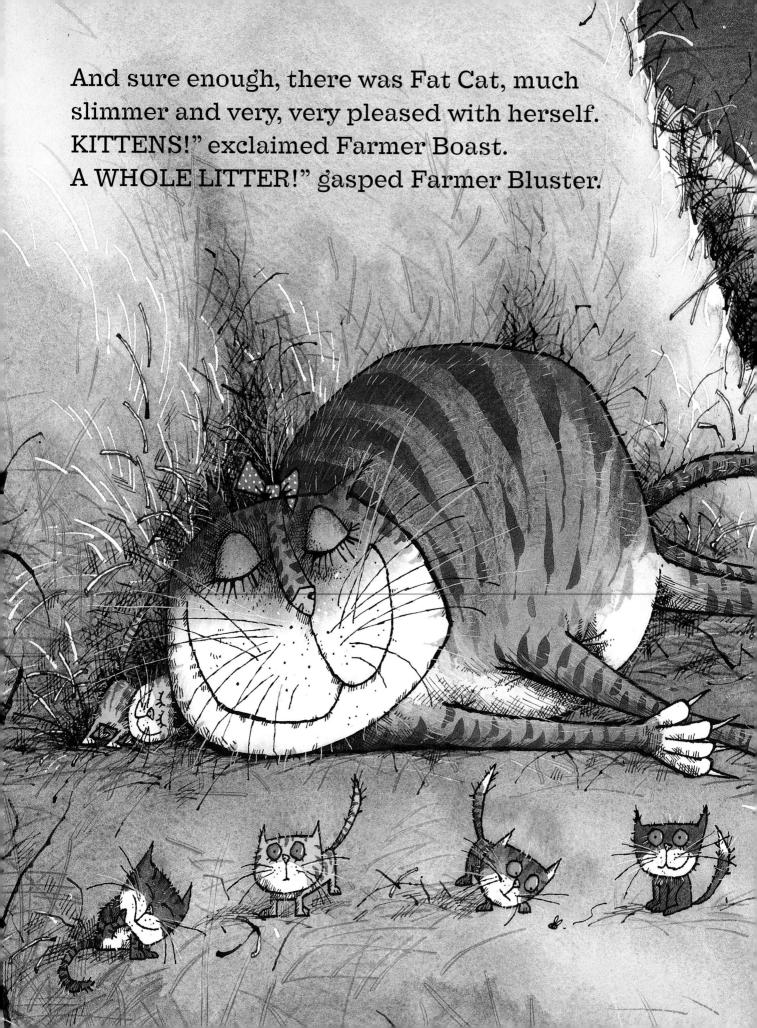

"Now you can have foolproof
mouse catchers, too," beamed Farmer Smart.

Soon the kittens grew into fat cats themselves,
and the fields of Farmer Boast and Farmer Bluster
looked every bit as good as that of Farmer Smart.

But secretly all three farmers thought his fat cat was the best!

To me, she'll always be Fat Cat.